WEEKLY READER BOOK CLUB PRESENTS

The Trouble with Santa

By Betsy Sachs

Illustrated by Margot Apple

A STEPPING STONE BOOK

Random House 🏠 New York

This book is a presentation of Weekly Reader Books. Weekly Reader Books offers book clubs for children from preschool through high school. For further information write to: **Weekly Reader Books,** 4343 Equity Drive, Columbus, Ohio 43228.

Published by arrangement with Random House, Inc. Weekly Reader is a federally registered trademark of Field Publications.

Library of Congress Cataloging-in-Publication Data
Sachs, Betsy. The Trouble with Santa (A Stepping stone book) Summary: When Billy Getten's class puts on a holiday play he learns how different cultures celebrate winter and wonders if there really is a Santa Claus. 1. Holidays—Fiction. 2. Winter—Fiction. 3. Schools—Fiction] I. Apple, Margot, ill. II. Title. PZ7.S11853To 1990 [Fic] 89-24257 ISBN 0-679-90410-7 (lib. bdg.) ISBN 0-679-80410-2 (pbk.)

Manufactured in the United States of America 10 9 8 7 6 5 4 3 2 1

For Margaret R.,
who understood the spirit of giving;
and for Bill B.,
who knew about the loss of Santa.

1

"Billy," said Billy Getten's mother, "would you get in line with Sarah?"

Billy looked across the crowded shopping mall. Little kids were lining up in front of Santa's green velvet chair.

"What if someone sees me?" he asked.

"Tell them you're taking your baby sister."

Billy hoped his best friend, Howard, didn't see him in the Santa Claus line. Howard would tease him forever. "Do I really have to?"

"Yes. I want to run into that store and pick up a Christmas tie for Grandpa. I'll be right back." Billy's mother rushed off, and Sarah started to cry.

Billy took her by the hand. "Look, Sarah," he said, "you can see yourself in the store window." He bent down and pointed at their reflections.

"Oh! Me!" Sarah smiled and waved to herself. "Me! Me! Me!" She began making faces.

"Hey, Billy," someone said.

Billy stood up. It was Chrissy Breen.

"Hi," he said nervously.

Tall, skinny Chrissy Breen was in third grade with Billy. Chrissy was even worse in math than Billy, but she made great stuff in art class. "You talking to Santa?" she asked.

"No, my sister is."

"Yeah, it didn't seem like something you'd be doing."

"Nah," said Billy. But a part of him secretly wished he was going to talk with Santa. He used to like doing that. It made Christmas fun.

"Well, hello there," a voice said.

Billy and Chrissy turned around. Santa was right behind them. "How are you, Chrissy?" Santa said.

"Wow!" said Billy. "You know her name!"

"Of course. And you're Billy Getten."

For a moment Billy believed in Santa Claus all over again. His sister was looking up at Santa wide-eyed.

Chrissy peered at Santa too. "Hey, do I know you?" she asked.

"Sure you do, Chrissy. I'm Santa from the North Pole."

Billy liked Santa's big round face and bright blue eyes. If only, Billy thought, Santa Claus wasn't just for babies.

Just then Billy's mother returned.

Santa said, "Good to see all of you from Lee Avenue."

He patted Sarah on the head. Her eyes grew even bigger, but she didn't make a sound.

Santa smiled. "Well, I'd better get going."

Chrissy whispered over Sarah's head, "It's the ice cream man."

"Boy," said Billy. "Wait till I tell Howard!"

"Don't ruin it for him, Billy," Mrs. Getten said.

"Oh, he knows," said Chrissy. "He was the

one who told the whole class last year. Well, I've got to go. 'Bye, Sarah." Chrissy patted Sarah's head too.

Suddenly Sarah came to life. "Santa! Santa!" she yelled. "Santa! Wait for me!"

Billy's little sister strained to get away from Mrs. Getten. People started turning around to see who was screaming.

Mrs. Getten picked Sarah up. "You ready to tell Santa what you want for Christmas?"

"Dollies and trucks!" Sarah shouted.

Mrs. Getten kissed her. "Billy, wouldn't you go up with Sarah, just for a photo?" she asked.

"Not me, Mom," Billy said. "I'm in third grade, you know."

2

On Friday morning Billy stared out the classroom window at the bare trees. The sky was solid gray. He was watching for the first snowflake.

"All right, class." Billy's teacher, Mrs. Markum, was tall and thin and had a long black braid. "Everybody clear your desks."

Susi Garcia, the class brain, dropped her book. Everyone laughed.

"Nice noise, Garcia," Howard Rosa said. Howard and Billy were not allowed to sit next to each other in class. Mrs. Markum thought they fooled around too much.

Mrs. Markum said, "Every year the third grade puts on a holiday play for the school.

This year I want to do something different."

Billy tried to remember what last year's third graders had done. He couldn't.

"Now that Thanksgiving is over, what holidays come next?" asked Mrs. Markum.

Several hands went up around the room. Billy's hand stayed down. He didn't want to be called on. He hated talking in front of the class. It made him nervous.

"Howard?" Mrs. Markum said.

"Christmas."

"Good. Any others?"

Matthew Swick raised his hand.

"Yes?"

"Hanukkah."

"And what happens for the Hanukkah celebration?"

"A candle is lit for eight nights in a row," said Matthew.

"Do you know why?"

"The Jews only had enough oil in a container to last one night, but it lasted eight. So when we light the candles, we think of that miracle."

"Right," said Mrs. Markum. "Anyone else?"

Susi waved her hand back and forth in the air. "I know one! I know one!" she called.

"Good, Susi. Tell us."

Susi stood. "My grandmother always gets a piñata at Christmas." She sat down.

Mrs. Markum nodded. "In traditional Mexican homes, for the eight nights before Christmas a piñata is broken."

"What's a piñata?" Howard yelled.

"It's a stuffed paper toy," said Susi. "Sometimes it's in the shape of a bird or a donkey. Inside there's candy and prizes."

"The piñata is hung from a rope and each child tries to break it with a stick," said Mrs. Markum.

"You wear a blindfold when you try to hit it," added Susi. "It's fun."

Mrs. Markum nodded. "Celebrating in the winter happens in many ways. It goes back to the time of the cave men."

"Hey, did they believe in Santa Claus?" Howard shouted.

Everyone giggled. Mrs. Markum laughed too.

"Does anyone know what the winter solstice is?" she asked.

There was no answer.

"It's the shortest day of the year," said Mrs. Markum. "Our part of the earth is tilting away from the sun, so we have less daylight. The cave men used to think that the sun was running away when the days got shorter."

"Big babies!" shouted Mark, the tallest boy in class.

Mrs. Markum said, "On the shortest day of the year, many countries celebrate with light. It helps you to feel happy when it's so dark and cold outside. Tonight I want all of you to find out if your parents or grandparents were born in another country. We're going to learn how people around the world celebrate the winter. Then we'll use that information for our play."

Billy studied the sky. Snowflakes were finally starting to fall. He really hoped he didn't have to be in the play. He hated acting in front of people worse than talking in front of people. It really made him sick.

The next day Mrs. Markum said, "Let's go around the room. I want to hear what you learned about your families' holiday traditions. Billy, you start."

Billy took a deep breath. Whenever he was called on, he always forgot what he wanted to say. "My great-great-grandparents came from Holland. My grandfather says they don't have the same Santa we do. He's called Kriss Kringle there."

"Kriss Kringle!" Howard hooted. "Sounds like a cookie."

The whole class laughed.

Billy looked at the floor. He felt silly.

"That's enough, Howard," Mrs. Markum said. "Billy, did your grandfather say anything about Black Peter?"

"Oh yeah. I knew there was another part."

"Tell us about Black Peter."

"He's Kriss Kringle's partner. He wears a black cloak and brings coal to children who are naughty."

Susi raised her hand. "That's what Santa Claus does."

"Right," said Mrs. Markum. "Many of the winter celebrations have parts that are the same." Mrs. Markum smiled at Chrissy. "What did you learn?" she asked.

"I didn't learn anything. I already knew it."

"Well, tell us, please."

"My grandparents are from Sweden. They live with us."

"So you celebrate the feast of Santa Lucia?"

"Yeah. The oldest daughter in the house is supposed to dress up on Christmas morning and bring food and stuff into the parents' bedroom."

"You don't sound as if you like it."

Chrissy shrugged. "I do. It's just that no one else does anything like us."

"That's why we're doing the play, so everyone will learn about everyone else. Do you have a favorite part?"

"Yeah!" Chrissy laughed. "You get to wear this neat crown with real candles."

"We won't be able to use real ones, but we'll find some plastic ones that light up. Now Yuri, tell us about what happens in Russia."

Yuri smiled. "We have Grandfather Frost. He brings gifts from house to house."

"Very good! And Howard," Mrs. Markum said, "what did you learn about?"

There was no answer. Billy looked down the aisle.

Howard had drawn a mouse face on his hand. Howard's mouse squeaked, "I forgot!"

The class laughed, but Mrs. Markum didn't.

"Howard," she said, "I want you to find out. And wash your hands before lunch."

"Mrs. Markum," a girl named Anita said. "I know about Italy."

"Good, tell us."

"Instead of Santa, they have a lady named La Befana. She comes down the chimney just like Santa. She gives coal to bad kids too."

"Wonderful; we'll use her also."

After Mrs. Markum had asked everyone, she said, "We'll do a play using all the different celebrations. Everyone will be in it."

Billy groaned. Just the thought of being in a play made him feel sick. He remembered how he had thrown up right before the Thanksgiving play in kindergarten. Even now he hated to think about that day.

"Let's figure out the speaking parts," said Mrs. Markum. "First, I need the cave man."

Matthew's, Peter's, Mark's, and Chrissy's hands all waved in the air. "Me, me, me!" they shouted.

Mrs. Markum shook her head. "Roger has a really loud voice. Let's let him do it."

"Boy," said Chrissy. "The only part I really wanted."

"Matthew, you'll talk about Hanukkah. Anita, I want you to be La Befana. Mark will be Santa. Yuri will be Grandfather Frost. Chrissy, you be Santa Lucia."

"I want to be a cave man," Chrissy said.

"I'm sure you'll be lovely as Santa Lucia."

"Billy, you be Kriss Kringle. And since you and Howard are buddies, Howard can be Black Peter."

Billy felt his stomach jump. He didn't want to be acting in front of a whole bunch of people. Not even next to Howard. And most of all he didn't want a speaking part. He might throw up right onstage!

3

Howard and Billy were in their favorite seats at the back of the school bus. Chrissy sat across the aisle from them.

"I can't wait!" cried Howard, pounding the seat. "The play's going to be great!"

Chrissy said, "I wish I could have been the cave man. That would have been cool."

Howard turned to Billy. "Hey, do you know what Black Peter looked like?"

"No."

"Boy, I hope he dressed like a pirate. That's the kind of costume I want."

The bus crossed through the middle of town. Trees with holiday lights twinkled in the early darkness. A Santa stood on every corner. "I wish there was a way to get out of it," Billy said.

"There's just got to be," said Chrissy.

"How?" Billy looked across at her.

"Get your mother to write a note saying you aren't allowed to be in plays."

"She'd never do that," said Billy.

"I could write it, but I bet Mrs. Markum would know my writing."

"You guys are such babies! What are you afraid of?" said Howard.

"Nothing," said Chrissy.

"Yeah," said Billy. But he knew it wasn't true.

"All you have to do is walk out onstage and say your stuff in a very loud voice. It'll be a cinch," said Howard.

Sometimes Billy hated his best friend.

"What good is a play about people celebrating around the world?" said Chrissy. "I mean—who cares?"

"You guys are just chicken!"

The school bus stopped in front of Billy's driveway. He and Howard and Chrissy jumped off.

"Bye-bye, babies!" Howard shouted.

Billy didn't say good-bye. He started toward his house.

"Hey, Billy!" Chrissy yelled. "Wait."

Billy stopped halfway down his driveway.

Chrissy hurried to catch up. "Could I borrow the math problems to copy? I'll bring them back tomorrow."

"Yeah, okay." Billy opened his backpack.

"Thanks," Chrissy said. She tucked the notebook under her arm. "I can't believe what a jerk Howard is sometimes."

"I know," said Billy. "Believe me!"

Inside Billy's house the kitchen was warm and steamy. There was chicken soup cooking on the stove. Billy's dog, Stewie, wagged his tail and sniffed at Billy's shoes.

Sarah was in her highchair. She was playing with a banana on her tray.

Billy dropped his backpack on the kitchen table and petted the dog. Stewie was named after Billy's grandfather.

"Hi there." Mrs. Getten smiled. "Want some hot chocolate?"

"Nah," said Billy. He slumped in a chair and watched his mother feeding Sarah.

"How was school today?"

"All right, I guess."

"What's wrong?"

"We have this dumb play we're putting on."

"I heard you talking to Grandpa about it last night. It sounded nice."

"Yeah, well, I don't really want to be in it."

"Oh, Billy, you'll have fun."

"No, I won't. I don't even believe in Santa anymore, and Mrs. Markum wants me to be Kriss Kringle. What fun will that be?"

4

Late Sunday afternoon Grandpa Stewie lifted his jacket off a peg in the hall. "Anyone for fresh air?"

"Okay," Billy said. He and his parents were visiting with Grandpa and Nana.

Out on the back porch Billy waited while Grandpa Stewie filled his pipe with tobacco. It was six o'clock and already too dark to see the stream beyond the pine trees.

"Sure do miss those long summer days," his grandfather said. A match glowed briefly between Grandpa Stewie's full face and chubby hands. Then the flame went out.

Billy sniffed the sweet-smelling pipe smoke

as it drifted away. Up above the pines he could see the stars.

Grandpa Stewie started slowly down the steps. "Let's go over to my shop."

Billy liked his grandfather's workshop. It was a little brown house off by itself at the edge of the yard. A path led up to the door.

Grandpa Stewie turned on the lights. "In you go."

Inside was a square room with a wood-burning stove in the corner. Billy could smell fresh wood and burned wood and turpentine and paint. Pencil drawings were tacked to the walls. Shavings covered the floor.

Billy sat on a pile of boards and picked up a curl of wood. He hung it over his nose. "What are you working on, Grandpa?" His grandfather was always making something.

Grandpa Stewie rested the pipe on his worktable. "I want to carve some blocks for Sarah." He handed a plain wooden cube to Billy.

"You made a set for me when I was a baby," said Billy.

Grandpa Stewie reached for a piece of

sandpaper and smiled. "You still have those?"

"Sure. Well, except for the one Stewie ate."

His grandfather shook his white head. "That dog. He's something else."

"Yeah, I was really mad at him for that."

"I just hope I get these done in time," Grandpa Stewie said. "There's always so much to do before the holidays."

"Grandpa?" Billy twirled the shaving around his finger. "Can I ask you something?"

His grandfather glanced up from sanding. "What's that?"

"How come everyone says Santa's real and he's not?"

Grandpa Stewie sighed. He put down one block and picked up another. Slowly he lowered himself into an old wooden rocker. "That's not easy to answer."

"Why not?"

"Well, it's complicated. There's not really a guy in a red suit at the North Pole—"

"Isn't that a lie then?"

"Let me finish, now." Grandpa Stewie scratched his neck. "You ask tough questions, kid. You know that?"

Billy smiled. He really liked his grandfather. "Just the facts, Jack. Just the facts."

Grandpa Stewie chuckled. "Well, when you're little, it's the only way adults know how to tell you about the spirit of giving. As you grow up, you come to understand Santa's more a feeling than a real person."

"What's that mean, 'spirit of giving'?"

"You give a gift to a friend and don't expect to get one in return. Or you make peace with someone you've been angry with. It's being kind when you don't have to."

"But Santa's just a made-up story. Right?"

"Hard to say. Almost every country has a legend about a person who gives gifts. All those legends started somewhere."

"Yeah," said Billy. "We talked about that in school."

Grandpa Stewie struck a match and held it up. "I like to think that when we're generous, a spark of Santa comes alive inside each of us. Maybe all our sparks together bring Santa to life each year."

"That's pretty nice, Grandpa." Billy blew out

the match that Grandpa Stewie held up to him.

Suddenly there was a knock. Billy's grandmother stuck her head in the doorway. "Doesn't anyone in here want dessert?"

"Yes indeed!" Grandpa Stewie pushed himself up out of his rocker. "We're just having a little man-to-man talk."

Billy followed his grandfather back across the yard. Grandpa Stewie stopped to light his pipe one more time. Billy watched the tiny flame push up against the darkness. He shivered when the wind blew it out.

5

The next day Mrs. Markum asked Billy's class to push their desks to the back and sides of the room. Everyone made lots of noise shoving desks across the floor and banging them up against the walls.

"All right," Mrs. Markum said. "That's enough. I want everyone to come sit in a circle on the floor."

Billy sat next to Chrissy. Howard sat next to Billy.

"Today," Mrs. Markum said, "we're going to work on decorating the stage for our play." She began to unroll a large sheet of heavy white paper. "Chrissy, come up and help me," she said.

Chrissy held one end of the roll. It was as tall as she was. Mrs. Markum opened it all the way to the other side of the room. A faint picture was penciled on it.

"Can you see the drawing?" Mrs. Markum asked them.

"There's a Santa," Susi said.

Yuri pointed. "There's some reindeer."

"And a sleigh and packages," Anita said.

"The art teacher did the drawings, but we have to color them in," said Mrs. Markum.

"Coloring's for babies," Howard said.

"No, it's not," said Chrissy. "It'll be fun."

"First," said Mrs. Markum, "we'll color and cut out the figures. Then I'll ask Mr. Downey to glue stands on the backs of the cutouts. We'll place them against the blue curtain at the back of the stage. It'll look like Santa is riding his sleigh across the sky."

"Let's make silver stars to hang on the curtain," said Chrissy. Everyone thought that would be pretty.

Mrs. Markum cut the roll into sections. Then she handed out colored pens and crayons. Soon everyone was coloring away.

Howard and Billy each got a reindeer. Chrissy had the moon and the stars.

"This is boring," Howard said to Chrissy.

"No, it's not," Billy said.

"Being Black Peter in the play is much more important than this," said Howard.

"You think you're so great!" Chrissy said. "You're doing that reindeer all wrong."

"So?" said Howard. "It doesn't matter." He pressed hard on the brown crayon and ignored her.

Chrissy snorted. She turned to Billy. "Could I show you something?"

"What?" said Billy.

Chrissy took Billy's crayon and started coloring the reindeer with long gliding strokes. She left some places empty. They looked like white spots on the reindeer's back.

"Wow," Billy said. "That looks nice."

Billy colored exactly the way Chrissy had. His reindeer began looking soft and furry.

The bell rang. Mrs. Markum said, "If you want to keep coloring and eat lunch in here, you may."

By the time the bell rang again, the class

was almost finished with coloring and cutting. Mrs. Markum stood the Santa, sleigh, and reindeer cutouts up against the desks.

"They look great," Mark said.

All the rest of the third graders thought so too. It didn't matter that chocolate milk had spilled on Santa's legs or that Chrissy had colored a smile on the moon. Chrissy said, "The moon is always smiling when Santa comes to town."

Everybody laughed at Howard's reindeer. "Its head looks like a duck's," said Yuri.

"We need a reindeer with a red nose to lead the sleigh," Mark said.

"Let's pick one," said Mrs. Markum. "Then we really must get back to schoolwork."

Chrissy pointed to Billy's reindeer. "I think that one's the best," she said.

Everyone agreed. Billy couldn't believe it. All afternoon he kept stealing looks at it. He was glad Chrissy had shown him that little trick with the crayon.

6

It was the day before the play. Mrs. Markum had Billy's class practice onstage one last time.

"Pretend I'm the audience," she said. "Go through the entire play without stopping. If you make a mistake, keep going. All right! Lights! Cameras! Action!" Mrs. Markum cried.

Billy watched from the side of the stage as Susi Garcia stepped forward. "Good evening," she said in a shaky voice.

"Louder!" Mrs. Markum yelled.

"Good evening," Susi began again. "Today is—" She stopped. "Today is the—"

"Susi, what's wrong?" Mrs. Markum came down the center aisle of the auditorium.

"I just forgot what I'm supposed to say. I knew it this morning."

"Susi," Mrs. Markum said gently. "Don't worry. I'm sure you'll remember tomorrow. Read the lines from your piece of paper. Let's keep going."

Oh no, thought Billy. If Susi forgot her speech, how would he remember his? He took out his crumpled piece of paper and studied the words again.

Mrs. Markum walked to the back of the auditorium. A group of kids was standing there. They were supposed to come down to the stage one by one.

"Mrs. Markum!" Chrissy yelled. "Roger's doing the cave man all wrong! He's not supposed to wiggle the club."

"I'm the cave man!" Roger said. "I can do what I want."

"Yeah, but the way you're doing it looks stupid."

"Chrissy," Mrs. Markum said. "The cave man is Roger's character. He gets to do it his way. Let's keep going. We don't have all day to fool around."

The rehearsal went on. Mark got sick and had to go to the nurse's office. Susi forgot her lines again and started to cry. While Mrs. Markum was talking to her, Howard pushed Yuri into the reindeer cutouts at the back of the stage where they were standing.

"Watch out!" Chrissy screamed.

Everyone jumped out of the way as the reindeer crashed to the floor. Santa fell on his face.

"Okay!" Mrs. Markum shouted. "Class dismissed, except for Howard, who's staying to help me fix this mess."

That night Billy lay on his bed, thinking about the play. Stewie's head rested on his stomach.

"I just know it's going to be awful," Billy said.

Stewie wagged his tail.

Footsteps came up the stairs. "Billy?" called his mother from the hall.

"Yeah?"

Mrs. Getten opened the door. "Come on

down to the den. I want you to try on your costume."

Billy rolled onto his side. "Do I have to?"

"Yes, I want to do the hem."

Billy followed his mother. Stewie followed Billy.

"What's wrong?" Mrs. Getten said over her shoulder. "You've been so grumpy."

"I still don't want to be in the play."

"Stop worrying."

In the den Mrs. Getten handed the long red robe to Billy. He pulled it on. It had a hood with a white tassel on the end. "Howard keeps bragging about how great he'll be in the play," said Billy.

"I bet he's just as nervous as you are."

"He sure isn't acting that way. He's not acting like my friend, either—just like a real jerk."

"Maybe he'll get better once the play is over," Mrs. Getten said. "Let's put the whole costume on you. I want to see how it looks."

Billy pulled on the white wig. Mrs. Getten arranged the hood of the robe over it.

"Very nice," she said. "Stand on the step-stool so I can mark the hem."

Billy looked at himself in the mirror. He really did look like Santa.

"Now, don't move."

Just then Sarah ran past the door. Suddenly she was back. "Santa!" she cried.

Billy's father was right behind Sarah. "I can't keep up with this kid," he said. He lifted her onto his shoulders.

"Down!" she shouted.

Billy didn't know what to do. He was afraid to say anything.

"Say good night to Santa," Billy's mother said. "It's time for bed."

Sarah made a face as if she was going to scream. But then she said in a soft little voice, "Good night, Santa."

Billy waved. Sarah waved back.

His mother and father took Sarah to her room. Wow, thought Billy, that was close.

When his mother came back, she said, "Oh, Billy, Sarah was thrilled."

"Yeah, did you see her face?" said Billy. "She really thought I was Santa."

"You were wonderful." Mrs. Getten gave him a hug. "What a gift to her that was."

"Huh," said Billy. "I didn't think of it that way."

7

The next morning when Billy's mother opened his door, he pulled the covers up to his ears. "I'm sick," he said.

Mrs. Getten felt his head. "You're fine," she said. "It's just a case of stage fright."

Billy dragged himself out of bed. He was slow getting dressed and even slower eating his breakfast. He missed his bus.

"I'll drive you around the block so you can catch it," his father said. "Just get your things."

"But I don't feel good."

"You're all right." His mother zipped up his parka.

"How come I don't feel all right?"

"Once the play is over, you'll see." She handed Billy his costume.

"Remember the last time I had to be in a play?" said Billy. "Right before, I threw up. Maybe I will again. Onstage!"

"You were in kindergarten and you had the flu."

Billy trudged down the snowy driveway. He climbed in the front seat of the car. His father backed out onto the road and drove down the street. Before long they caught up with the bus. "We'll see you later," his father said. "Have fun! Plays are supposed to be fun."

"Not for me." Billy climbed out of the car.

The bus was crowded. Only the seat next to Chrissy was empty.

"Hi," she said.

Billy saw that she had her costume in a clear plastic bag on her lap. "I think I'm going to throw up," he said.

Chrissy laughed. "Me too."

"My mother and father didn't believe me."

"Mine either. I should throw up onstage," said Chrissy. "Really."

"Me too."

"Want to?" Chrissy laughed again.

"Yeah, that would be great." Billy smiled.

"I bet if you did and I did, some of the other kids would too. That always happens."

It sounded like a neat idea. The only problem was, talking about it made Billy feel better.

When they got to school, Billy started toward Mrs. Markum's room. Roger ran up to him in the hallway. "You gotta see this!" He was laughing.

Billy followed Roger to the boy's room. The door was open. He heard laughter coming from inside.

"Geez, it's green," someone said.

"Look at that. You can tell it was toast," someone else said.

Billy stopped in the doorway. Someone had been sick all over the floor.

"Howard barfed," Roger said.

"I'm getting out of here!" shouted Mark. "It smells!"

Mark, Roger, and Matthew pushed Billy aside. "Don't go in there," Matthew called over his shoulder.

Billy heard a groan. He stepped inside. Howard was leaning over one of the sinks. A string of spit hung off his chin.

Billy couldn't believe the other kids. Even

though Howard had been a jerk lately, Billy knew he couldn't leave his best friend. "You want me to get the nurse?" he asked.

Howard kept his head down. "No," he moaned.

Billy took a paper cup and put some water in it. "Wash your mouth out. My mother makes me do that."

Howard filled his mouth with water, then spit it out. "Thanks." He let go of the sink. "I don't know my part," he groaned.

"You don't! What happened?"

"I forgot it on the bus. Then I got sick thinking about it." Howard took another sip.

"I missed the bus thinking about it. Can you imagine if we all forget our parts?"

"Mrs. Markum will kill us," said Howard.

"Can you imagine if we all barf onstage?" Billy started laughing. "That's what Chrissy wants us to do."

Howard laughed a little too. "Oh, don't make me laugh. It hurts."

"Sorry," said Billy. He took a deep breath. "Come on. I'll help carry your stuff."

8

Billy peeked out from behind the closed curtain. He wanted to see if his parents and Nana and Grandpa Stewie were in the audience. Billy could just make out Grandpa Stewie's white hair. That meant they were all there.

The lights went off and the curtain opened. Then the music teacher began playing the piano. Half the kids in the play came down the center aisle from the back of the auditorium. Each one wore a red felt hat and a green felt cape. Each carried an unlit plastic candle.

When they had climbed the stairs and were in place onstage, Susi Garcia stepped forward. She turned the bottom of her candle. A tiny light glowed at the top.

In a very loud voice she said, "Good evening. Today is December twenty-first. It is the shortest day and the longest night of the year. Today is the first day of winter. It is called the winter solstice. Ever since the beginning of time, people all over the world have used light and fire to celebrate the winter." Then she stepped back into line.

There was a rumbling sound. Roger Smith, dressed in a fake leopard skin, came down the aisle dragging a club. He stopped to shake it at the audience. The children giggled. Roger dragged his club up the stairs of the stage.

"I'm a cave man looking for the sun," he said. "It must be lost because the days are so short. I build fires so the sun will know how to find me."

People in the audience laughed. There were a few whispers.

Roger said, "Fire is good because it keeps wild animals and bad spirits away. It helps me cook. I like fire. It makes me feel safe and happy."

Roger moved into the line of other third graders. Lots of candles were turned on around him.

Next Matthew stepped forward. "Long ago the Jews did not have enough oil to light the temple. At this time of year a candle is lit for every night to celebrate the miracle of Hanukkah."

Matthew lit his candle and moved back into place. One by one, eight lights went on around him.

Then Mark came down the center aisle. He was dressed in a long red robe and a pointed cap. "A long time ago in Turkey a man left gold on poor people's windows. He became known in Europe as Saint Nicholas. Today he is called Saint Nick or Santa. Lots of countries celebrate winter by remembering him."

Yuri was dressed in a fur hat, a blue cloak, and boots. He wore a long white beard and held a small tree with lights on it. Yuri talked about Grandfather Frost of Russia.

From backstage Howard and Billy and Mrs. Markum watched La Befana and then the other Santas come onstage. When it was Howard's turn, Billy whispered, "You're not going to throw up, are you?"

"I don't think so." Howard put a coal sack on his back. He marched out onto the stage.

"I am Black Peter, the best friend of Kriss Kringle!" he roared.

What? thought Billy. That wasn't part of Howard's speech!

"If you're not good little boys and girls," Black Peter said, "I'll put coal in your stockings." He strolled across the stage. "And I'll tell my buddy Kriss Kringle about you." Howard made his fake black eyebrows go up and down.

Billy couldn't believe how much Howard was changing his lines. Mrs. Markum was going to kill him!

Howard turned to the side of the stage. "Yo! Kriss!" He waved Billy onstage. The audience laughed.

Billy took a deep breath and walked onstage. He held a small lighted tree in one hand and a tiny bell in the other.

"I am Kriss Kringle from Holland," he said.

"I climb in the windows of the good children's homes. I leave a tree and lots of presents for them. You'll always know I've been there when you hear this." Billy tinkled the bell. "But when you're not good, my best friend, How——I—I mean, Black Peter—tells me."

Howard put his arm around Billy's shoul-

ders. Together they walked to their places in the line.

Billy took another deep breath. His speaking part was over. He felt wonderful.

From backstage Mrs. Markum whispered, "One, two, three." All of the candles were turned off. Now the hall was dark except for the red exit light way in the back.

Everyone waited for the next person to speak. Nothing happened. Billy couldn't remember whose turn it was. Then all of a sudden he heard a murmur in the audience.

Down the center aisle came Chrissy. She was wearing a white dress with a red sash around her waist. Circling her blond hair was a thick green wreath with five flaming candles in it.

"Oh no!" gasped Mrs. Markum.

There was not a sound in the audience. Very slowly and carefully, Chrissy walked up the stairs. "In Sweden," she said to the audience, "we celebrate with food and drink and song. . . ."

Billy hardly heard Chrissy's words. He was thinking she looked beautiful with candles in her hair. The glow they gave off reminded him of stars. No wonder all the countries used light to celebrate, he thought. It really did make you feel happy.

Then Billy heard Susi say, "Thank you for coming to our play. We wish you lots of light and cheer during your winter celebration." One by one the third graders turned their candles on.

Mrs. Markum hurried out onstage. As the overhead lights came on, she smiled quickly at the audience and took the wreath off Chrissy's head. She let Chrissy blow out her candles.

There was a sigh from the audience. Everyone clapped.

Mrs. Markum and the class took a bow. There was more clapping, and the curtain closed.

9

Later that night Billy held the door open while his parents brought a Christmas tree into his grandparents' house. They set it up in front of the living room window.

"Okay. That's it for tonight," his mother said. "We should head home."

Billy's grandmother hugged him. "Good night," she said.

Billy kissed her. "Where's Grandpa?" he asked.

"He said he had something to do in his shop."

"I'm going out to say good night."

"Tell him to come in. It's getting late," Nana called after Billy.

Billy headed across the driveway. His feet made crunching sounds against the hard dry snow. He stopped to watch his breath float away into the night. In the sky the stars glowed faintly like candles.

The lights were on in the workshop. Through the window, Billy saw his grandfather's white head bent over the workbench. Billy rapped on the glass, and Grandpa waved him inside.

"Will you look around for some fresh sandpaper, Billy?"

"Sure." Billy opened a cabinet door. "There's some in here."

"I'm not going to have Sarah's blocks done in time for Christmas," Grandpa Stewie muttered.

"Nana says you should come in."

His grandfather only nodded. "I should have stayed at home and worked on them. But then I'd never have seen your play."

"Did you like the play, Grandpa?"

"You were a wonderful Kriss Kringle. I liked that little gal at the end, too."

"You mean Chrissy? Yeah, even Mrs. Markum wasn't too angry when she saw Chrissy's metal headpiece was meant to hold those candles."

"You mean that wasn't planned?" Grandpa looked surprised.

"Nope."

Grandpa Stewie smiled and shook his head. "I liked all those Santas standing up there together."

"Me too," Billy said.

"I wouldn't have missed it for the world."

"Grandpa, you know you could have my blocks to give to Sarah."

Grandpa Stewie put down the block he was polishing. "That's mighty nice of you, young man."

"But I want Sarah to think they're from Santa."

"Seems like the Christmas spirit finally hit you, eh?"

"I think so," said Billy.

"Billy?" Nana's voice called across the driveway. "Your parents are waiting."

He opened the door. "I'm coming."

Nana called again. "Your dog wants to go out."

Billy stood in the doorway. "I'll watch him, Nana."

Stewie bounded out of the house. He began rolling in the snow.

Billy's grandfather said, "If we use your blocks, all I'll have to do is clean them up a little." He gave Billy a hug.

"I'll bring them over tomorrow and help," said Billy. "Good night, Grandpa." He shut the door to the little brown house. Outside, he waited while his dog sniffed the snow.

Billy looked back at the workshop window. There, framed like a picture, was his white-haired grandfather. There was a pipe in his mouth. He had on his old red jacket, and he held a box of toys in his arms. Billy saw him reach for the light switch, and then the picture disappeared.

"Oh wow!" Billy laughed out loud. Grandpa Stewie looked just like Santa Claus.

"Hey buddy, you know what?" Billy petted

his dog. "Tomorrow I'm going to fix up my old blocks for Sarah. I'll make stuff for my parents and Nana and Grandpa and Howard and Chrissy. And I'll even make something for you."

About the Author

When BETSY SACHS was in second grade, she really did meet a Santa who knew her name and what street she lived on. Even now, she keeps a Santa Claus statue out all year round, because Santa is her favorite hero. Betsy Sachs says she wrote *The Trouble with Santa* because she "wanted to share the joy of always believing in him." She lives in Waterbury, Connecticut.

About the Illustrator

MARGOT APPLE has illustrated literally dozens of books for children, including *The Boy Who Ate Dog Biscuits,* also a Stepping Stone Book. She lives with her husband in the countryside near Ashfield, Massachusetts, where she would like to make presents for people but doesn't have the time. She's too busy illustrating books.